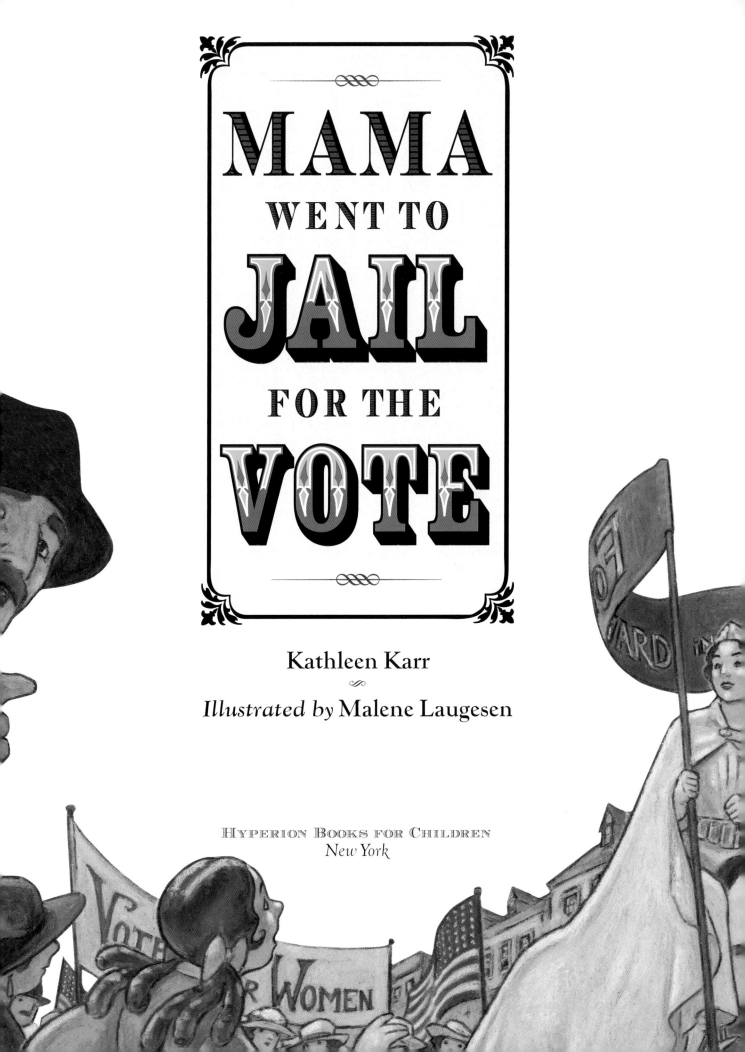

MAMA
WENT TO
JAIL
FOR THE
VOTE

Kathleen Karr

Illustrated by Malene Laugesen

HYPERION BOOKS FOR CHILDREN
New York

In memory of my mother, Elizabeth Szoka Csere—another feisty lady
—K.K.

For my mother, Karen, who has the courage to fight for her dreams
—M.L.

Text copyright © 2005 by Kathleen Karr
Illustrations copyright © 2005 by Malene Laugesen

Printed in Singapore
First Edition
1 3 5 7 9 10 8 6 4 2
This book is set in Kennerley.
Designed by Elizabeth Clark
Reinforced binding
ISBN 0-7868-0593-5
Library of Congress Cataloging-in-Publication Data on file.
Visit www.hyperionbooksforchildren.com

"I hate these bloomers, Mama!"

Mama didn't even blink. "Nonsense. Now you look like a modern girl, Susan Elizabeth."

"I'd rather have a cowboy suit," I insisted, "or an Indian outfit, with a bow and arrows."

That made Mama frown. "You know I don't approve of violence, Susan Elizabeth. Besides, bloomers make a statement."

I groaned. Mama liked to make statements. Papa and I learned to live with them. Mama was a modern woman. She was a *suffragist*. That meant she was fighting for the right of women to vote.

The fighting part interested me. "A bow and arrows would make a statement, too, Mama. I'd aim mine straight at those politicians who keep women from voting!"

"We shall never attack with anything but votes, Susan Elizabeth! I believe in fighting for the right to express our views, but not with violence." Mama was firm. "Votes are better than bullets or arrows, any day."

"Yes, Mama." I sighed.

It was hard to understand this voting business. Once a year Papa stuffed his
pockets with cigars and said, "Don't wait dinner for me. I'll be with the gentlemen
at the saloon to see how the election turns out."

I turned to Mama. "Will you carry cigars and hang around the saloon when
you have the vote?"

Mama was shocked. "Certainly not, Susan Elizabeth! That, indeed, is one of
the things we women wish to change!"

"Oh." I thought about that. "Then why would you want to vote?"

"Because women are in chains, daughter!" She swept her arms around. "We are half the population of this great nation, yet we haven't any say in how it's run. That's why we want the vote! Someday we'll be able to choose our own candidates." Mama stood very tall. Her eyes gleamed. "Someday we may even be able to choose a *woman* as a candidate."

My mouth fell open. "Like you, Mama?"

Mama only smiled a secret smile.

After that, Mama's crusade became more exciting for me than playing cowboys and Indians. Sometimes Papa grinned and patted Mama when he got home from work. "How many votes did you round up today, my dear?" he'd ask. That usually made Mama sniff and storm off. But mainly Papa ignored the entire business and inquired about dinner.

"Did you help Cook to make the lovely roast I smell tonight, Susan Elizabeth?

It's so nice to know that some women are still keeping the home fires burning. Always remember the important thing, daughter."

"What would that be, Papa?"

"Why, keeping your papa happy, of course. Women were meant to be an ornament to man, and to comfort him after his labors."

"Are you sure about that, Papa?" I asked. But I fetched him his newspaper and slippers anyway.

I didn't really mind making Papa comfortable, but it was much more fun helping Mama fight for the vote. Parades were the best. Mama got to sit on the back of a big white horse to lead a parade down Pennsylvania Avenue—right past the Capitol, all the way to the White House.

"Let me ride with you, Mama," I begged. "Please!"

Mama leaned down from the saddle. "I'm sorry, darling, but you'll have to wait till you're a little older."

"Oh, pooh!"

Mama trotted off. She certainly looked impressive on that horse, sitting as tall and proud as any Indian princess. But the tomatoes the boys on the street threw didn't match her fancy dress very well. Neither did the raw eggs.

That got me mad, and I found some eggs to throw right back at them. I wasn't sure it was the proper way to fight, but since none of us had the vote yet, it was the best I could do.

After a few years, when the parades didn't seem to get them the vote, Mama and her lady friends decided to take their issue right to the top—to the president himself. The ladies said he was too busy fussing about some war across the ocean in Europe to listen to them. From what I'd seen, peeking through the fence, I thought maybe he was too busy playing golf on the White House lawn.

Mama started to spend her days right in front of the White House gates. Now she was more than just a suffragist.

"Think of me as a soldier guarding our frontiers, Susan Elizabeth."

"Is that what a picket is?" I asked.

"Yes." She nodded. "I'm holding messages for the president himself to see."

"I want to be a soldier, too, Mama!"

Mama gave me a kiss. "You may come and watch after school, dear."

I did come every day after school, but I began to think that President Wilson needed new glasses. Mama stood there clear through the winter and into the spring, too. He still didn't seem to notice her. When summer came, I took up the fight and picketed with Mama.

I'll never forget the day President Wilson finally took notice. The ladies had given me my very own flag to carry. I liked the colors a whole lot—purple for dignity, white for purity, and green for hope. I liked taking a rest from picketing to play in Lafayette Square across the street. But best of all, I liked marching with my flag.

"You're part of the great Army of the Future now, Susan Elizabeth," Mama told me. That made me feel fine. I hoisted my flag higher.

Suddenly, along came a new parade. It was made up of another army: soldiers

and sailors going off to the Great War across the sea. Their uniforms were brand new, and their rifles were shiny. The men halted outside the White House to listen to President Wilson. All at once, everything kind of exploded. When the shouting began, Mama shooed me across the street.

"Susan Elizabeth, I'm ordering you to the rear of the lines."

I retreated to the top of Lafayette's statue to get a better view. Those soldiers and sailors didn't seem to appreciate Mama's Army of the Future at all.

"Don't give up the fort, Mama!"

Shots rang out, the way they do on the Fourth of July, but this time the rifles weren't pointed at the sky. They were pointed at the banners. I started worrying about Mama.

Next, the police arrived. And there was Mama being hauled away in handcuffs!

"Mama!" I gasped. "You really are in chains!"

I raced across the street and pulled at the policeman holding Mama.

"Arrest me, too!" I demanded. "I'm part of Mama's army."

That big policeman only laughed and said, "I'll let you go, lady. You need to look after your spunky little girl."

Mama stared him square in the eye. "Being imprisoned for my beliefs is looking after my daughter's future!" She bent down to kiss me. "Don't worry, darling, the battle may be lost, but the war isn't over. Tell Papa not to wait dinner."

Mama never made it home for dinner at all. Mama went to jail for the vote. Papa wasn't pleased. Even Cook's fricasseed chicken didn't help.

I wasn't hungry, either. It was hard getting those chains off my mind. When Papa and I had gone to the police station, they'd told us we couldn't visit Mama, but she could write us one letter a month . . . if she was good.

"Is Mama a criminal, Papa?" I asked.

"I should say not! She was merely expressing her American right to protest."

"If she has the right to protest, why hasn't she the right to vote?"

Papa set down his fork to pull at his collar. "Well, now—" He cleared his throat. "Voting polls are not the nicest places for proper ladies to be."

"Neither is jail, Papa. And if ladies went to vote, wouldn't the polling places become proper places to be?"

Papa didn't answer. He just shoved his plate away and waited for Mama.

Papa waited a long time, but I got tired of waiting. I was part of Mama's Army of the Future, and Mama had only ordered me to the rear. She hadn't ordered me out of action. I knew how to make banners, so I did.

Then I went downtown and stood in front of the White House. President Wilson must have gotten new glasses, because he saw *my* sign quickly enough. He even walked to the gates and poked his head out to talk to me.

"What's this all about, little girl?"

"My name is Susan Elizabeth, and I thought presidents could read, sir."

"Indeed." He looked at my sign again. "And do you believe women should have the vote?"

"Yes, sir, Mr. President, I do." I pointed at my bloomers. "These are modern times, aren't they? You need all the help you can get to run our great country. Women should be helping you, not sitting in jail. Especially not my mama!"

He sighed. "I suppose you're right, young lady. I've already planned a few words for the Senate on the subject. But thank you, Susan Elizabeth." President Wilson tipped his hat and turned back to the White House.

It certainly was nice having Mama home again. Six months is a very, *very* long time. Mama didn't like jail or its food one bit, but she was a real soldier.

She accepted her punishment. Then she went right back to the war, right back to carrying banners in front of the White House. I did, too.

I guess the president's talk to the Senate didn't help. Two entire years passed after President Wilson won his Great War before Mama won her war. Women had the vote at last!

I was allowed to go with her and Papa to a genuine voting precinct. I
true: she didn't need any cigars at all. All she needed was a ballot and
and a good idea of who might make our great country even greater.

I loved the beautiful silver JAILED FOR FREEDOM pin Mama received from the National Women's Party for going to prison.

Mama pinned it on her dress like a medal. "Someday, Susan Elizabeth, this pin will be yours. If . . ."

"If what, Mama?" I asked.

"If you keep fighting the good fight. If you faithfully promise to vote in every single election once you are old enough."

I crossed my heart. "Mama, you needn't worry about that. I promise!"

HISTORICAL NOTE

Suffragists began organizing for the woman's vote much earlier than the twentieth century. The story truly began at the Woman's Rights Convention held in Seneca Falls, New York, in July 1848. This was planned by Elizabeth Cady Stanton, Lucretia Mott, and several of their friends, who were frustrated by their lives as middle-class wives.

As a result of the publicity that the Seneca Falls convention received, ideas about the "New Woman" spread like wildfire. Soon Susan B. Anthony joined Stanton in the cause. Amelia Bloomer invented a new article of ladies' clothing—the bloomer—which scandalized the country. Anthony and other women began touring the United States giving lectures on women's rights.

Still, the Congress in Washington expressed no interest in creating new laws extending enfranchisement to women. By the early teens of the twentieth century, women became more frustrated, and even more vocal. Alice Paul, who had learned a few protest techniques while helping the suffragettes in Great Britain, moved to Washington and formed the National Woman's Party. It was under Alice Paul's leadership that the suffrage parade of March 1913 was organized. It was under Paul's leadership that picketing began before the White House in January 1917.

Yes, women were the very first picketers at the White House! For their efforts, they were initially ignored, later attacked, and finally jailed—some for as long as six months. Many of the imprisoned women went on hunger strikes and had to be force-fed. Eventually, all 168 of them were pardoned by President Woodrow Wilson, and he agreed to support their cause before Congress.

The Nineteenth Amendment to the Constitution of the United States, which gave women the right to vote, was finally passed and ratified, and was signed into law on August 26, 1920. In November 1920, women in our country were permitted to vote in a national election for the first time.

"JAILED FOR FREEDOM" PIN, 1917

THE NINETEENTH AMENDMENT TO THE UNITED STATES CONSTITUTION

The right of citizens of the United States to vote shall not be denied or abridged by the United States or by any State on account of sex. Congress shall have power to enforce this article by appropriate legislation.